Knitting Nell

by Julie Jersild Roth

HOUGHTON MIFFLIN COMPANY  BOSTON 2006

For dear loves, John, Elsabet, and Joren.
And for Ann Rider, for her extraordinary nurturing, kindness, and wisdom.

www.houghtonmifflinbooks.com

The text of this book is set in Diotima.
The illustrations are watercolor.

Library of Congress Cataloging-in-Publication Data

Roth, Julie Jersild.
Knitting Nell / Julie Jersild Roth.
p. cm.
Summary: Everywhere Nell goes, she works on her knitting, quietly observing life around her, until one day she enters one of her creations in the county fair, and receives rewards beyond her dreams.
ISBN 0-618-54033-4
[1. Knitting—Fiction. 2. Fairs—Fiction. 3. Friendship—Fiction.] I. Title.
PZ7.R7323Kn 2005
[E]—dc22
2004015779

ISBN-13: 978-0-618-54033-4

Printed in China
SCP 10 9 8 7 6 5 4 3 2 1

This is Nell.

She knits . . . a lot.

 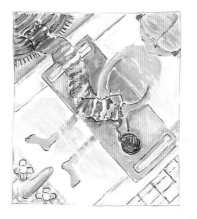 

A boy named Danny Tucker once told her she had a voice like a cricket with a pillow over its head. And she believed him.

So Nell doesn't talk a lot.

Sometimes she knits at the park so she can listen to the trees.

Her friends often come by to chat, and Nell listens to them.

As Nell listens, she knits a blanket for her aunt's new baby.

She knits lots of socks and hats and mittens for the Children's Home.

She knits more socks and hats and mittens for people in a country far away whose leaders are at war.

She knits matching
scarves for Grandma
and Grandpa,

a scarf for Mom,

and Dad,

and her brother . . .

and somewhere in the midst of all of this, Nell makes a beautiful sweater for herself

and decides to enter it in the county fair.

Let's go see that new movie "Monster Mixup."

I hear that is way too scary!

I, personally, would LOVE to see "Princess Peanut" or "Dogs in Love."

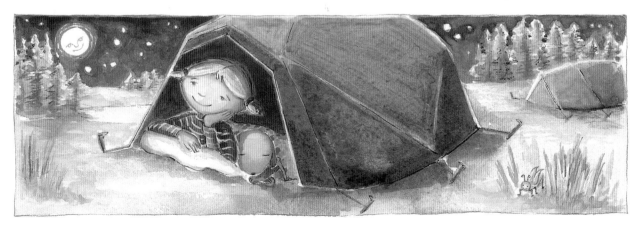

Weeks later . . .

Nell and her friends are very excited about the annual county fair.

At the end of the day, everyone looks forward to the champions' ceremony under the big tent.

Nell and her friends find seats together.

"Friends of Green County . . . it is time for the announcements of the GRAND CHAMPIONS!"

"Most obedient dog . . .
Pickles!"

"Prettiest cow . . . Lucy!"

"Best sheep . . . Daisy!"

"Most creative seed art . . .
Danny Tucker!"

"Tastiest cake . . . Andy Harper!"   "Best pickles . . . Dena Jones!"

"And best knitting . . . Nell Nielsen!"
Nobody is really surprised when Nell wins first prize for
her sweater,

but for all those gifts of socks, and hats, and mittens, she is also awarded a beautiful, special medal from the mayor of her town.

Nell's family is so proud, and her friends are amazed.

Yarn:
red, pink,
blue, yellow
needles:
sizes
9, 10, 11

Nell still knits a lot,

and she listens a lot,

but now, with her happy cricket's voice, Nell talks a lot, too.